The Little Bat who Loved Halloween

By
Stephanie O'Connor

For
Isabella and Matthew

Once upon a time,
there was a
little bat
who
loved Halloween.

He lived with his parents in a deep cave
on the side of a steep mountain, and the
mountain looked upon a great forest.

Every day. the family flew
through the forest, from dusk
until dawn hunting for food.

The little bat was a happy little bat.
But it did worry him that he had not yet
seen the forest in the daytime.
He wanted to see how the birds and
animals that awaken in the morning
spend the day there.

Now it happened that one day,
in the season of Halloween,
that the little bat, who knew nothing about
the fun that Halloween brings,
listened round-eyed with wonder to the other
bats who knew all things about Halloween.

When he heard that Halloween was a special time for bats, and that boys and girls dressed up like goblins and witches, and thought that the forest was full of spooky things, the little bat made up his mind to have fun too.

"How **amazing** it must be!" he thought.

"Halloween in the FOREST!"

"Come on," said his mother the very next day, as they were flying towards their home in the cave. "It's time for bed. We must be quick, the sky is growing bright, and I can already see the sun coming out to look for us."

The little bat slowly fluttered along behind his mother, and Father Bat came up right behind them.

They had been flying through the moonlit forest all night long, zipping effortlessly through the tree branches in the dark, as they chased the little insects that come out after the sun has gone down.

But now that the night was over, and it was time to go home, the little bat flew slowly, holding back from his mother, and with a very cross look on his face.

"Hurry up!" said Father Bat.
But the little bat did not fly faster.

Little Bat was cross because today
was a special day. Today was

Halloween!

And he was thinking about how he
would love to spend the daytime in
the forest on Halloween.

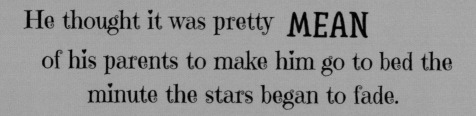

He thought it was pretty **MEAN**
of his parents to make him go to bed the
minute the stars began to fade.

And on

Halloween of all days!

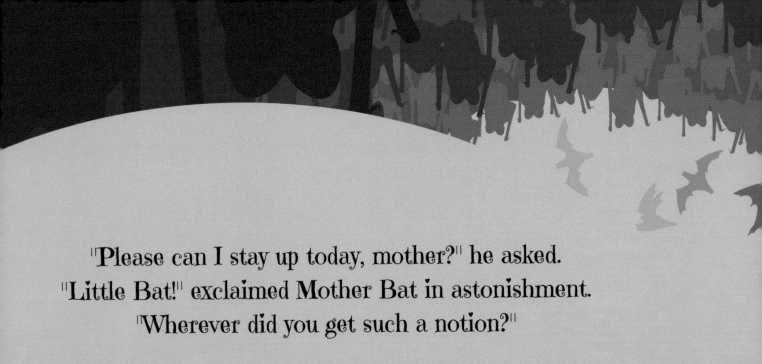

"Please can I stay up today, mother?" he asked.
"Little Bat!" exclaimed Mother Bat in astonishment.
"Wherever did you get such a notion?"

"Absolutely not!" said Father Bat to
him, when they reached the cave.

"But why? It's Halloween after all?" he asked as they hung themselves up.

"Because you wouldn't like it, for one thing. The forest in the daytime is not for us - we are night creatures," his father replied.

"And you're far too young," answered his mother. "If you were to go, how would you find your way home through the forest? You might get lost."

Little Bat was very upset.
"I know my way through the forest," he insisted.
"Please," he begged, "I've never been to Halloween in
the forest in the daytime."
"Now, Little Bat, be good and don't mention it any
more!" said Mother Bat.

His mother spoke sternly, and Little Bat burst
into tears. He was very fond of getting his own
way, and when he didn't get it, sometimes he could
be a little naughty.

He coaxed and coaxed his mother and father to let him stay up, but it didn't make the slightest bit of difference. So he folded his wings to go to sleep in the cosy darkness of the cave, hanging, head downwards, close to his parents.

But as hard as he tried, he just couldn't fall asleep!

"Stop fidgeting," whispered Mother Bat to him,
when Father Bat was asleep.
"I'm not tired," Little Bat answered.

"GO TO SLEEP!" snapped his father,
for he did not like to be woken up.

"NO!" thought Little Bat, I'M NOT."

And as soon as his parents were asleep,
and when all was still,
he crept softly out into the morning night.

Little Bat flew away from the cave
feeling very brave indeed.
He felt like a big-boy bat!
"I can take care of myself," he thought
happily to himself. "even if it is daylight!"

He made up his mind
that he would spend Halloween
day in the forest,
and that was that!

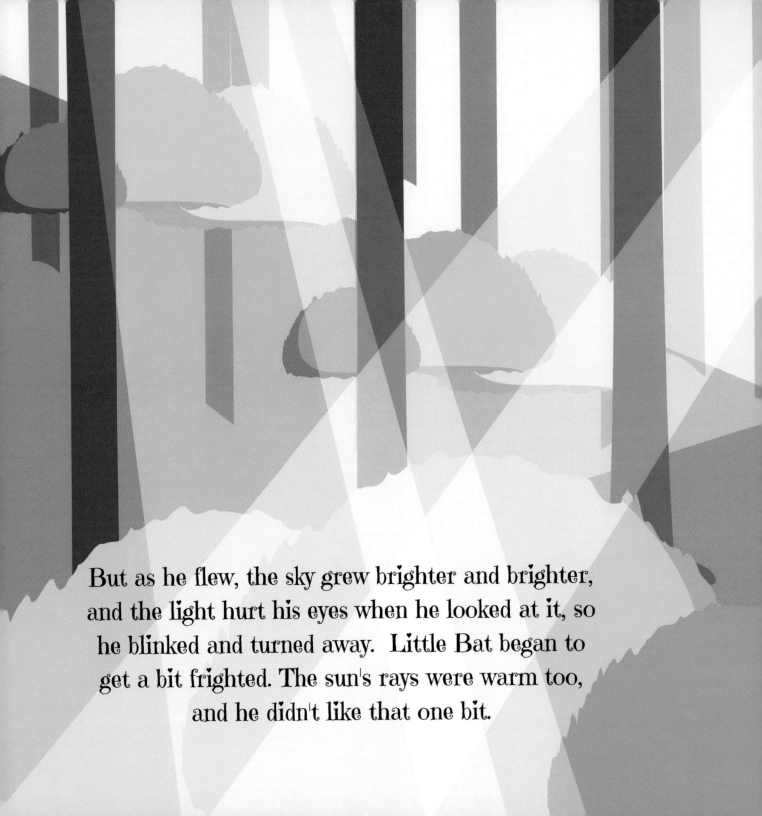

But as he flew, the sky grew brighter and brighter, and the light hurt his eyes when he looked at it, so he blinked and turned away. Little Bat began to get a bit frighted. The sun's rays were warm too, and he didn't like that one bit.

Soon he reached the forest, which
he knew so well, and his heart began
to beat with excitement.

"Hi!" he shouted in greeting
to all the forest creatures.

But wait, what's all that racket?
he wondered.

During the night the forest is a lovely quiet place, but now,
during the daytime, it was as noisy as could be! Songbirds had
awoken and were singing to their heart's delight. It was all
fascinating to the little bat, but the noise hurt his ears!

"Shhhh!"
he said, coming towards the birds.
"You are singing too loudly!
What's the sense in shouting like that?"
"Excuse me!" said a songbird. "We are singing to
the sun as it comes up to warm us."
Even so, Little Bat didn't see the sense of
shouting. The night-birds never made such a mad
fuss over the moon, and surely the moon was just
as important as the sun!

The bird was cross at the interruption.
"What kind of bird are you anyway - to quiet
our joyful singing?" asked the bird crossly.
"I'm not a bird!" answered Little Bat.
"Well, you fly, don't you?" said the bird.

"Yes, but I'm a bat - look," he said. and he fluttered
around until he reached a branch where the bird could
see that his wings had no feathers like hers. Instead,
they were black and seemed to grow on to his legs and
have hooks on both ends. Not only that, he didn't have
a beak - instead, he had a tiny little nose and ears.

Just then, Little Bat sensed something scampering over the ground. He turned to look for whatever it might be, but the creature was too quick for him. Suddenly a sunbeam came slanting through the forest, and Little Bat was dazzled by the light. He panicked and started to fly, but he bumped into a tree.

"Oh, my!" said the bird as she watched Little Bat swiftly tumble down to the ground where he landed directly on the grass.

Luckily an owl saw it all, and swooped swiftly down from the tree to help.
"Oh no!" Little Bat cried. "I'm usually very good at flying, but the sunbeams are not like moonbeams, and I don't like that! And I feel too warm!"

"Come on! Come on!" called the bird, and the other animals of the forest gathered around Little Bat. Two rabbits, who were feeding near by, came scampering along, to see what all the fuss was about. A fox, a hare and a toad too.

The owl introduced everyone, and they were all such a friendly lot, that Little Bat soon forgot his worries.

"What are you doing in the forest in the daytime Little Bat?" the squirrel asked.

"He's come to scare us!" said the rabbit.

Little Bat thought this was a very surprising thing to say. "Why would you say that?" he asked.

"Oh, don't you know? Nighttime is the fun time at Halloween," said the rabbit. "And Halloween night is the time when the bats come out to scare everyone"

"The same way we all did," said the spider crawling down from her web.

"Yes as Halloween approaches, it's the spookiest mystery of all! Why some of us, like bats, toads, wolves, owls and spiders, remind everyone of this ghostly night," agreed the toad, who was already wearing his big Halloween hat and didn't look scary at all!

Little Bat was sad.
"I've made a terrible mistake. I should go home, bats like me don't belong in the forest in the day time and especially at Halloween! I'm no use here today!"

"What nonsense!" his new friends said.
"We still have to get ready for the party, perhaps
you could help us with that?"
"I would love to," said Little Bat excitedly.
"What do I have to do?" he asked.

And so it was, that all day long the forest creatures rushed back and forth, waving and talking hurriedly to each other as they got ready for the Halloween party and fun they were to have that night. And everyone was excited.

The Hedgehog gathered autumn leaves of the forest trees lying thick on the ground to make costumes of green to scarlet, orange, and brown.

Birds practiced their song.

"Oh, dear, Oh, dear!" cried the ants, hurrying around. "There's so much to do!"

The chipmunks and squirrels hurried along, and carried nuts and seeds for the Halloween feast. While the rabbit whisked her long tail and scampered off through the grass.

From morning until night the chirping and humming of the happy creatures, mingled with the rustle of the autumn leaves. Little Bat helped where he could, and would have been hard to find a happier bunch of creatures than in the forest that Halloween day.

Finally the forest was ready, and the animals were waiting for it to get dark so they could have fun. And, then, after supper, when the sun had gone to bed, it got dark.

"Good gracious!" cried a bird. "The glowworms are beginning to light. It's nearly sunset. All who are going to come to the party on Halloween night best be on their way."

"But what of Little Bat? Who is to take him home?"

"Never worry about that," replied the owl. "I will take him home."

The owl flew with the swiftness and little bat followed close behind. The moon rose high, while one by one the stars came out as they sped across the sky.

The owl seemed to know the exact way to the cave, for just as the moon rose, the little bat glided down to the cave entrance. Little Bat just had time to say "Thank you!" before the kind creature was off, and he was left behind.
"Enjoy Halloween night." the owl called from the sky.

Just then, Little Bat heard his
mother.
"Little Bat!" she cried. "We have been
so worried!"
She looked very anxious and ready to
scold him for sneaking away!
But seeing his little worried face, she
pulled him close, and wrapped her
wings around him in a big snuggle.

Back in the cave, Little Bat told
his parents about the wonderful
day he had in the forest.

"It was hot, and I didn't like the sun one bit!" he said,
"but I never had so much fun."
His parents listened to his story and when it was over
Little Bat promised never, ever, to sneak away again
and to always tell his parents where he was going.

"You must be sleepy now, Little Bat," said his mother, "it's time for you to go to sleep."

He was a very tired little bat, but he said "NO! I won't go to bed!"
Mother and Father Bat looked at each other without speaking, then smiled.
"Very well," said his father.

"It is Halloween night after all. And this is our night!"

The End

BOO!

Printed in Great Britain
by Amazon